# The Taryn Files

*By Shanna Bryant*

Printed in the United States of America

First Printing, 2019

Published by Pencil Werk Press

ISBN: 978-0-9960374-9-5

Pencil Werk Press
P.O. Box 452
Paw Paw, Mi 49079

Email: pencilwerkpress@gmail.com

Written by: Shana Bryant

**Cover art and design by Dan Monroe**

**Cover photos courtesy of**
Patrick Dove/ Dove Photography
Jonathan Doyle Photography

**Hairstylists**
Tisha Irby
Danielle Jelks

For Ma,
For having my back from day one, I would not be here if it weren't for you. You are my ride or die. My biggest fan in anything I do. I love you.


For Mike Brainard,

You've hung onto every word during the process of the Taryn Files. Even tuned in for the next tale. You may live clear across the country but I always felt you were right next to me when I'd be editing. You wouldn't let me give up and bail when I'd hit a block. You always reminded me that I got this. Thank you so much for being such a grand friend whom never let go of my hand. I love you. My biggest fan!


For a good friend,

I miss our traveling days when I'd write a tale and read it to you as we drove all over this country, or when we pick apart a story when stuck in traffic. But mostly, you were the one who helped me release Taryn. I thank you so much for listening. Eight years we worked on this together. That's eight years of listening! Thank you and I love you.

Every woman has a Taryn in her, in some way, form, or fashion. It's up to that beautiful woman when,   where and how she releases her Taryn. I didn't know I had a Taryn until a very special person in my life helped me discover her. Now, I don't see my life without her. She has brought out some of the best in me. She was my shadow during my spiritual awakening as a woman. She empowers me, enlightens me, and she lets me get to escape sometimes to just go play.

So, I share my Taryn with you.

-Shanna

Shanna has been writing since the tender age of 6 years old. Her first published piece was a letter she wrote to The Lansing State Journal about what she wanted to be when she grew up. Writing has always been a great sense of expression for her. She's offered her writing skills to The Michigan Bulletin as its Medical Reporter. She also has studied Journalism and Creative Writing at Lansing Community College.  She enjoys writing erotic short stories and watching her fan base grow by the day. She believes as long as there is lust and sensuality amongst us, there's a story to tell. The Taryn Files is her first publication with Pencilwerk Press……..but not the last.


You can also find some of her poetry and short stories at Writerscafe.org.

# Taryn's Intro



The flash of black strobe lights, disco ball spinning, smoke machine producing clouds of mystery, dueling dj's, juggling bartenders, and a shoulder to shoulder dance floor with the exception of one small space is a recipe for  an eventful night. She's wearing a brown oriental printed gold trimmed corset with a drop key pendant nestled in her appetizing cleavage. Her large curled hair is semi-pinned up giving a succulent glimpse of her soft shoulders and a lean back peppered with curious tattoos.

She seems to hold a slight gravitational pull towards anyone within her reach. All of the beautiful women want to huddle near her. Bask in her glow. Follow her lead. Learn her. Unbeknownst to them, all of the men begin to slowly orbit this elegant yet exotic woman. They want to get closer.
"Who is she?"
"Where did she come from?"
"She got a man?"
"Who cares? Look at her! She can't be single! No real man would let THAT go! Damn, son!"
The men continue to whisper and wonder about their new creature.
She seems to float with the music. Her hips glide symmetrically with the lingering rhythm. Her rose dusted cheeks dimple deep when she flashes a smile. She's taking ownership of this festive facility and all who occupy it. She's tucking it deep within her heart…… and her corset. Her moves compliment the dj's magnificent art. Sipping an amaretto sour through a red straw, she looks over her soft shoulder and winks at the dj. He nods and spins another. Nobody knew what that connected communication meant. And I doubt anyone ever will. The lights hit her subtle makeup presenting the question," Why paint the peacock? "
Her drink is getting low. She naturally sways towards the bar. Like breathing, she straddles a stool and another drink almost magically appears. She pulls out a cigarette and places it loosely between her rose red tainted lips. Before she can reach for her lighter, a flame sparked right before her very eyes.
As she leans to light her cigarette, she's thinking, "Who is he?"
"Where did he come from?"
"Does he have a woman?"
"Who cares?"
His eyes met hers. He snaps the zippo away and leans in three inches from her diamond studded ear. She slowly inhales his cooling yet striking scent.

"Your name misses?"
 She licks her full lips, held out a carefully manicured hand, creates a smirk, and says,
*"Taryn"*

The next morning…….. The weary siren opens her eyes and her thoughts to the alarm clock screaming,
***"Little Red Corvette".***

Her personal theme song, she lays on her back staring at herself through the mirror on her ceiling.

*"Baby, you're much too fast".*

Two days on. One day off. That's her party schedule. Cabaret and sin for two days then rest and refresh for one day.

*"You need a love that's gonna last".*

She exhales long and soft, spins her legs over the bed and places her pedicured bare feet on the cool and flat hardwood floor. First things first on one day off are to dismiss whoever's lying on the other side of her bed. In black boy cut shorts and a magenta pink camisole, she leans over to view this creature that fell victim to her sex. Her sexy. Her sexuality. A faint, immature, yet all too familiar aroma met her nostrils, Corona and cheap menthol cigarettes.

"Putz" she says under her breath.

Feeling her nipples rise and erect with the cold morning chill, she puts on a fleece pink and white polk-a-dot robe. She nudges his foot with her knee.

"Wake up. You got to go".

She crosses her stylish studio apartment, opens the door, and waits as her guest dresses. He stops just shy of her and the door but she quickly says, "I'll call you later"

This always cues her overnight suitors to exit stage right. She closes the door, posts up on her suede couch and grabs the remote. She heard there was a Golden Girls marathon on today. Two days on. One day off.

## *Intravenous Love*

### *A different kind of love affair........*

*"Come on Jay, please! You're the only one I trust when it comes to this stuff. Please!"*

**O**ne day off was coming to a close as Taryn begins her weekly "wraparound her finger game with her almost non-existing yet this part of her world revolves solely around best friend, Jay, who has what she needs. He holds the key to her imprisoned inhibitions. He is the guard that keeps her alienated animalistic. He loathes and lusts her caged casual encounters. He despises that treacherous transition. It's a bittersweet thought. He has to guard all of it. Not just the up and away or the funny freaky fun and last and always least, the dogged down dip. Jay is the guard to all of it.

"I don't know, Taryn," said Jay titfully teasing. "I know, he giggles. But it only takes me two."
"Jay!"
"Alright, alright, but can I pick one?" he asks with a childlike inquire.

Hesitantly, she replies, "Ok, ok."
Jay turns his back to her. He begins to tinker. Her heart begins to beat double time. Her mouth begins to salivate. A gleeful glimmer forms in her bright brown eye. He turns towards her and lifts up. She looks up, at it. He flicks it. Tests it...................................................
A quick and quiet calm hovers between the two friends. Taryn exhales low and steady, her eyes meet Jay's.

"Good?" he asks

"Good," she replies with a smile.

# *Entertaining*

**The things Taryn does to prepare for a night of entertaining........**

Taryn rips and roars from closet to closet in a black tank top and grey sweatpants. Jay is at her computer quietly replying to his "pick of the litter". That's what Taryn calls it. He gets to choose who his best friend will invite and endure.

"It better be a good one!" she sings cheerfully from her wall to wall mirrored vanity room.

"Oh I think this one's going to be perfect." replied Jay with a coy smile. She emerges seductively in the doorway of the computer room. She then spins around displaying her fashionable ensemble: a long strapless, deep plum colored, satin dress. Black four inch open toe heels compliment her small and soft feet. A waist high slit displays a full and supple caramelized thigh. In one hand she holds a bottle of Stella Rosa red wine. In the other hand, purple fuzzy bunny cuffs.

"Well how do I look?" she asks. Jay swallows hard and mentally searches for words. Quite a difficult task right at the moment,

"You look sensational", as Taryn's cheeks blush a shy blissful pink. She lowers her eyes in that sweet modest way that always drove Jay crazy in love.

"Thanks," she whispers. Another quiet and quaint calm lingered between the two best friends. He stands from the rolling computer chair, walks slowly over to Taryn. He stops close enough to smell her Obsession perfume and red wine on her breath. She looks up at him. Her bottom lip quivers. Jay recognizes this as one of her nervous actions. He puts both hands on her slim waist and gently squeezes. He meets her nose to nose.

"You're a goddess. You're going to do just fine."

"Ok," she replies and nods her head.

"One more?" he asks.

She straightens her posture, gains her composure, and replies,

"Yes, one more."

**"Ding Dong"**........


**H**eadlights illuminate the darken foyer as Taryn sways towards the door. Her heart skips a beat when she hears his car keys jingle from the other side of the door. She never knows why she gets nervous right before entertaining guests. Never fails though. As she reaches for the doorknob, she steals one more glance of herself through a diamond shaped mirror hoisted on the fireplace mantle to her right. She replays Jay's voice in her head, "You're a goddess."
She opens the door and leans all of her weight on her right hip giving an outright gorgeous view of that thigh. "I've been waiting for you," she says as her eyes move from the top of his head full of wavy dark          hair. She opens the door and leans all of her weight on her right hip giving an outright gorgeous view of that thigh. "I've been waiting for you," she says as her eyes move from the top of his head full of wavy dark hair.
A thin goat-tee with matching slivering sideburns sets off his thin pink lips moistened by a bubble gum tongue. She doesn't quite get to view the rest of his package before a lean and fit arm wraps around her yearning hips. In one quick swift move, he's hooked her, twirled her back against the door, slamming it shut. Her body instantly recognized what was happening and went with the flow of his body. She raised that exposed thigh and wrapped the whole limb around his waist. She can hardly breathe with his face filling hers with kisses-a-plenty. Instantaneously, she hears his jeans unzipping and her black silk panties rip in two. Before the torn lingerie float to the floor, she snatches them out of thin air, shoves them into his mouth, and finally throws her head back as he enters her. Heartily hard and getting to girth, he also lets out a grunt, a sign that says she's still got it. She holds on to his shoulders by digging her nails into his milky skin. This opens up her sugar walls a little more. His rock hard ass muscles start to flex. Flex hard and swift. He holds one of her arms up over head still pressed against the door. Hands meet and fingers intertwine, His breathing now hard and rapid, she whimpers. It's happening. He's unloading inside of her. Right before the last drop is deposited deep up into her guts, she peeks over his muscular shoulder. Her eyes are darting in the dark, left to right.
"Where is it? She asks herself. Where are you? It's happening. Where are you?"
Just as he explodes verbally and from his internal to her's, she sees it, the little red dot at the end of the hallway.
"Damnit, Jay! She fusses mentally; you better have gotten all of that!"

# The Palm Spring Bay Fling

## *VACATION!!!........*

It can get downright BORING with the same people, clubs, and trends where Taryn resides. Sometimes, she needs new scenery. New light but most importantly, a place where nobody knows her. A place to leave her calling card.

"Jay, pack your shit. We're going to the bay for the weekend. Pack EVERYTHING," she said all in one breathe.

"Yep, yep, be there in 15," replies Jay.

Taryn begins to pace in her bedroom. She absolutely hates packing. But she would commit fashion suicide if she just packed a random handful of clothes. She begins to pluck and pull any and everything from her closets. Opening and shutting dresser drawers, surveying both shoe nooks, and eventually deciding to pack her whole damn jewelry collection. If all else fails, she can always wear a pair of diamond earrings and a smile, wouldn't be the first time. Exactly 15 minutes later, Jay is letting himself in with his copy of the apt key.

"Taryn, it's me! I'm here!"

He walks swiftly across her studio apt and rounds the corner entryway to her bedroom. There he finds 9 bathing suits laid out quite neatly on the bed. Taryn staring at them from the foot of the bed.

"No! No! No!" Jay exclaimed irritated.

"We are not going to battle with the bikinis this year. Pack two, finish up in here, and meet me in the car. Now!" screeched Jay.

"I hate it when he's right," she whispers to herself and then packs 6 bikinis.

She exits her apt with a black rolling suitcase in tow behind her, a white mesh beach bag over her shoulder, an oversized bright white cotton floppy hat on her head, sunglasses shielding her eyes from the sun, a knitted black halter top loosely cups her perky twins, and a long flowing linen skirt concludes her favorite fun in the sun outfit. She only LOOKS pure and innocent in this get up. She loads up the backseat of Jay's convertible. Hops shotgun and before her seatbelt clicked, they've already gone 0 to 60.

At the "Under the Moon" soiree, Taryn makes eye contact with a sun stricken local from across the dance floor. A slow yet sensual and powerful bongo beat echoed off of the walls. She sways with the forbidden bass and saunters over to her prey. In an all-white, low cut, sun dress, she lets the hem brush across the sandy ground as he spins her around quickly and then dips her. Still suspended in air for the exception of his hand holding her by the small of her neck, he whispers,

"My place or yours?"

She brings herself back to her feet and bends over to brush sand off of her heeled sandal and to give a sneaky peek of her glistening cleavage. She slips him the key to her beach house rental. She pulls him so close that her lips brush across his as she says,"10:30."

She turns sways and saunters to the beat of the drums right out through the door. Jay picks her up in a nearby cobblestone alley and puts the pedal to the medal for their beach house. Twenty minutes later, the two friends part ways for a little bit.
 As Jay walks out of the back door, he calls back to her, "Good one?"
She replies back, "Very good one!"
He latches the backdoor as she opens the front door to invite her gentlemen caller inside. His eyes canvasses
her body. He's noticed she's changed into a black camisole with matching satin thong, covered by a sheer black robe. His blood races faster and faster raising the bulge in his pants when his eyes meet her small feet dressed in 4 inch stiletto heel.

*The Musician*



### *Sexy siren seeks something different........*

Taryn always, always makes sure she's remembered. Someway, Somehow, Yeah, that's a good way of putting it. But there's more to this sex kitten. More to this sensual siren, she's realizing she wants…..wants…well…she wants to mean something. Inspire. Motivate, and not always sexually.  She's got a soul like everybody else. Just nobody knows the humble and modest part of it. But God, how the hell does she share that? One day off has just began at 9:00pm on a chilly rainy Saturday night. Jay's at a gay couple's retreat with his on and off beau trying to find true love.  That leaves Taryn to herself, and by herself.  One day off, a day to reflect and rest. She decides to reflect with a walk on the square. She walks to her bay reading window and stares at the small raindrops hitting the panel quietly yet steadily. She thinks, "Rain. That's cleansing. It's also cold and wet. Better dress accordingly." Some things never change.

Across the square at the Rhyme and Reason Music Bar, a quiet loner rebel type bass player is sitting backstage in a chair kicked back against the wall balancing w/ one leg, strumming empty notes, yearning to write something new. Be more than just top billing on a marquee. All of the screaming purple mohawks, stage diving, and black lipstick on everybody is getting boring. Strumming, balancing, and strumming. A breath of fresh air, a muse, hell, maybe just another gin and tonic is what he usually has before he gets ready to perform. At least two or three back to back ends up being five before the curtain goes up.

Keeping up with the fashion and blending in with the crowd, Taryn walks into the Rhyme and Reason, folds her clear England style umbrella, unbuttons her full length black trench coat which a hostess with purple and green Shirley temple curls and cat eye glasses takes and seats her at a solo table in a far back dark corner. Before sitting down, Taryn adjusts her sleeveless pitch black pant suit so the wide leg pant would breathe freely as she sits. Twiggy style black sunglasses still rest on her face as she smiles at the waiter and orders an amaretto sour with a red straw. A black tribal medallion pendant drops to her cleavage. A piece she always wears with this all black outfit that matches a quaint onyx ring and black diamonds design her ear lobes. Reflecting incognito tonight she thinks as the lights went out, the crowd goes ape shit, curtain goes up, then a spotlight. Silence. Deathful silence. Taryn tilts her head for the awkwardness of the beginning of the show.  He strums the first note to a soulful but angry ballot. Then the tempo picks up, hits the roof, and fills the room. The lights. Oh my God, the lights. Glad she kept her Twiggy's on. Bright rave light sticks begin spinning. Entering, exiting, and crossing strobe lights. She sees the show through fragments of identifiable movements. But the bass player never makes another move other than strumming his instrument to the same rhythm. He never even opened his eyes. The rest of the band is rocking away. The song abruptly stops and all at once, the waiter sets Taryn's drink down, Taryn takes a drag from her cigarette, slides her sunglasses off, the bass player opens his eyes. Eye contact is made.

The bass player sprints off stage and through a back door that leads to a dark alley. He had to get air. He shook his head and shivered as he realized it's raining cats and dogs. Thought he saw……..something……out in the audience. Or was the booze just talking back to him. As two blonde bimbo groupies in sequined mini squirts asked if they could get in, he opened the door and motioned for them to come in. Before he closes the door, he sees an oversized umbrella, a black trench coat, and a lit cigarette turn around and walk away quickly towards the all night diner across the street. He barely maneuvers through traffic to catch up with her. Pouring rain and bright headlights blur his vision as he finally bursts through the diner's door. He frantically looks left to right. No sign of her. Then an older waitress with a bleach blonde beehive hairstyle asks.

"You play in that band across the street, don't ya? The bass player?" he shakes his head yes still out of breath. The vintage waitress cracks on her gum, reaches in her pocket, and pulls out a sticky note in the shape of a red heart.

"This is for you," she says, winks, and walks away.

I'm across the square, third floor.

Even though its only across  a small courtyard that everyone calls the square, it felt like light years as he climbed three flights of stairs, turned the corner, and find Taryn sitting on the steps. Cool and calm as a cucumber, hair, makeup, jewelry, and outfit still perfect. She's sitting on the steps with toned legs spread wide open. Her elbows resting on her knees her eyes fixed on him. He's soaked head to toe in black leather and suede. Still out of breath, he never takes his eyes off of her. She gestures for him to follow her into her studio apt. At first, he hesitates, but then walks through the door and she closes it softly, slowly locking it.

The studio apt was pitch black except for the lightening striking taking quick electrical atmospherically images of grey suede furniture, side tables and a winding staircase. Taryn walks with full stride across the wooden floor. Her heels clunk and tug at his heart at the same time. "Sit ", she says without turning around.

 He obeys. Heels clunking came closer to him. Her Obsession perfume lingered his nasal passage. He's now shivering as she hands him a towel and men's size lounge pants. She gestures for a trade his wet clothes for the dry ones. She turns and disappears into the laundry room. Then some tinkering in the kitchen and she returns with two black mugs of steaming tea.

She hands him a mug and slowly blows away the steam and whispers," Careful. It's very hot," then sits back on the love seat opposite of him.

The bass player finally gathers some gumption," Where did you come from? I mean, ummm, who are you?"

He is now stumbling over his own words. She crosses her thick thigh over the other and watches him over the rim of her mug. She wants to believe her nonchalant mild sexual charm is breaking him down slowly. She heard somewhere "less is more". Maybe, she inhales cooly, sits up, sets her mug on the glass coffee table, and stares at him. He follows suit.

"I believe we've been looking for one another for quite some time," she replies as she traces the rim of her mug with her index and then traces her bottom rose colored lip.

Thunder cracks through the black sky following another lightening photo shot of two bodies beginning to gravitate towards each other, slowly. The lamp flickers.

 "It's like you knew I needed something, new, you!" he said without breaking eye contact. Another roaring crack of thunder.

Taryn tilts her head softly, "Is that right?"

Lightning strikes again. Lamp shakes and shivers.
I'm not one for lyrical miracles and all but, we might be onto something," she replies with a whisper.
"Well I live for lyrical miracles and I think you're it," he replies.
He crosses the coffee table and kneels down next to her.
"Let me learn your body. Play its beautiful notes. Write its beauty all over my body, you, your body."
He caresses his hand up her leg to her mid-thigh.
"Needs to be beautified. Purified with whispers."
Both hands are holding her hips.
"I want to taste you. All of you. Mind, body, oh yes body, and soul as well."
That was it for Taryn. She'd found what she wanted as well. He unbuttons the bottom of her shirt and runs his hand across her navel. She tries not to swallow hard, tries to steady her breath. Give in to him, Taryn, she thinks to herself. He looks up at her. Let him sing to your body. Into your hazel eyes.
"What does T stand for?"
Another crack of thunder, the lamp bulb not only sizzles, and then sparks, finally shattering apart. Total darkness. Total silence. Just heavy breathing.
She throws her head back and whispers,
"Taryn."
He rips her shirt wide open. Buttons fly everywhere. Pitch black. There's a rustle and bustle. Lightning strikes revealing Taryn straddling her musician but her back is arched almost completely backwards as he grips her hips and burying his face in her lacy black bra. His biceps are bulging. Dark. Rain pounding on all window panes. Thunder shaking the Earth. Lightning strikes again capturing Taryn on her back, hair carefully laid off the side of the loveseat, her musician in between her legs, his face buried in her neck, his hand holding her up by her neck. He moans. She whimpers. Dark. Shattering thunder roar. Flash of his hands spreading her thighs. Darkness.
"Keep your heels on," he whispers into her quivering sugar walls.
Wind and rain take over the outside world as he dominates her insides. Flash. He pushes her face down into the loveseat gently but firmly. Darkness and silence falls upon the lovers for just a moment. Darkness. A hustle and bustle.
"Please?" she whispers. I have to. I want to. Please?"
"No, he gasps and moans. It's about……he moans…oh shit….it's about your body tonight."
He groans.
"Please", she begs breathlessly.
He moans louder. Lightning strikes a vision of her musician sitting on the loveseat, her on her knees, head bobbing up and down. He reaches for the back of the couch with one hand. Darkness. Moaning. Groaning. Flash. His other hand on her head aiding the rhythm. Pitch darkness surrounds the bodies.
"More!" she screams.
"Yes! Yes! He grunts.
His hand slaps her left ass cheek as he has her bent over the glass coffee table pounding her ass. Thrusting and groaning overpower the thunderous roars as both bodies hold onto one another giving into the explosion. Literal thunder and lightning accompany the musician, his muse, and their mind blowing toe curling climax.

# *The Thug*

## *Curiosity........*

They'd met once or twice in a quiet casual yeah-yeah-yeah-nice to meet you kind of way at mutual friends' house parties. He was a tall glass of cool chocolate milk. Oh no doubt about that. But the doo-rag, fitted baseball cap worn sideways, oversized white t-shirt, and jeans halfway down his butt is not her idea of an acquaintance. Hell, eighteen to twenty eight year old black guys have been brainwashed by television and social media. And, in her personal opinion, are not the best lovers. But this one was different.

Taryn went with Jay to run a few errands and ended up at a mutual friend's house. Taryn waits impatiently on a shabby couch in a tiny living room area with a small round wooden coffee table in front of it. She hates having to wait. So she scans the room for something. Anything to keep her mind entertained. A window with smoke stained curtains, an empty fish tank, two huge dog bowls (empty as well) with the names Bud and Weiser painted on them, and a staircase that she did not care to know where it lead to. She sits back on the dingy couch and waits for Jay. She only had her eyes closed for a split second when the......coffee table.......started......to vibrate?

"What the hell?" she whispered as she sat straight up at attention.

The next thing she heard were heavy black Timberlands booking it down the stairs. The doo-rag and baggy jeans stopped at the bottom of the stairs when he realized Taryn was sitting there. He flipped the extra swag switch on and strolled over to her and the vibrating table. He bent and reached over right between her and the musical coffee table. She went to move her feet out of his way but he grabbed both of her ankles with one muscular hand and grabbed his vibrating phone from under the table with the other.

"You're alright. You're good," he said.

And then gently places her black suede heels back in their original place. He walked back up the stairs and never looked back.

"Ahh shit," she said under her breath. Now I HAVE to divide and conquer that. A young black kid with......manners? I mean no bitches? No hoes? No slang? A polite gentile if you will?" Collecting her thoughts, phone, keys, and purse, she announces from the bottom of the staircase,

"Jay, let's roll!"

Taryn was quiet all the way home. But Jay knows. Jay knows her inside and out. And he knows how to handle it.

Not even an hour later, Taryn's standing in front of her full body mirror in the bathroom. She's tugging and pulling at her pink laced bra layered with a sheer and short sleeve button up blouse just a darker shade of pink, dark blue J. Glow jeans, no socks and pink pearled toes accents the term "precious pink". After applying some pink eye shadow, black eyeliner, mascara, and pink berry flavored lip gloss, she turned just to find Jay standing there with a new container of make-up removal. He hands it to her. Another familiar nerve racked action.

"You look like a $2.00 Amsterdam whore. You're thinking too hard. Talk to me."
The only time she gets into a thinking zone, she plasters layers and layers of makeup unbeknownst to herself. Jay leads her back to her vanity table chair with bright pink light bulbs lining the oval mirror. He bends over to her face and firmly scrubs off the "Miss Piggy" look.

"Jay, you know I'm not attracted to black guys. You know I get bored way too fast. And there's no emotion."

"You don't even have emotions in bed!" Jay shot back giggling.

"Don't hate the player, hate the game," Taryn replies with her head held high.

"You know what I mean Jay. Never a grunt or a moan, or even an, oh baby! Oh no wait, but if I yell out that I want to have his baby, he'll get rock hard and bang the hell out of my innards for Pete's sake," she says as she rolls her eyes in disgust.

So why again are you having him over? asked Jay,

"Because, she began. I don't know. A decent manner able black guy has got to be different from the other ones, right?"

"Possibly, replies Jay. "Or it could be the chase, he says as he spins her around to see herself in the mirror.

"My Gods and Goddesses", she whispers in shock. My makeup is perfect. Thanks, Jay!" Standing up behind her and joining her in their reflections, he readjusts her heart pendant and kisses the back of her neck.

"Let's finish getting ready," he says as he walks out of the room.

A half hour later, Taryn, Jay, and Sean are seated on the floor around the coffee table. Taryn had to sit on her hands like a first grader to disguise her shaking and excitement. She inhales quite deeply as Jay sends Craig into a new world, their world for the first time. Taryn thought for a moment realizing she didn't want to do this without Jay.

She turns to Jay, nod, and whispers, "You too."

 Jay's bright blue eyes glittered and quickly joined the tri-eclectic euphoria.

***Taryn also has a spiritual side to herself........***

# The Elements Part 1, Moon

***Moonstone brings passion........***

# Moon

Taryn also has a spiritual side to herself..... Once a year Taryn joins a cleansing retreat named Mount Monique. Like a tune up if you will. At the bottom of the mountain a camp director hands all retreaters a stone of some sort tied to a piece of twine and a map with instructions for every encampment. Opens the gate, wished everyone good luck, and Blessed Be.
After finding the first encampment, Taryn reads the instructions.

"Tie your stone to the tallest tree branch that is in the moonlight's beam. Lay on the slate rock and fall into a peaceful slumber as your body takes in the moon beams. Blessed Be."

Taryn follows instructions properly and lies down to fall into a slumber but sits up just as quick. She looks around to see if anyone was around, just her and the moon. She tinkers in her bag, waits for it, the euphoria has arrived. She closes her eyes and fully undresses. A strong but cool air drifts through her hair and whispers in her ear. The air kisses her warm lips. This force seems to wrap around her hips many times. She bends to all fours and it leans against her backside. Her hair is swirling around her ears. She inhales the sweet smell of the moon beams. Her body is also welcoming it as well. The forces seem to move up against her faster and faster. She throws her hair back as the movements were there, and then nothing. Her breath slows to calm, she lays her naked body in the fetal position on top of the sleight slab. She'd just made love to the moon.

# The Elements Part 2, Fire

*Be careful around fire........*

## Fire

$T$he next morning, Taryn is hiking Mount Monique with her pendant in one hand and a handful of curiosity about last night in the other.

"What in the hell happened last night," she asked herself.

But she continued the hike. It had been well past dusk when she noticed smoke coming from over the trees, and the base of a drum, Smoke, Drums and Smoke.

"Tie the pendant around the wrist of the Goddess of Fire and she shall protect and guide you through the hot dark night. Included was a black tie. Have the Goddess blindfold you and she shall guide you through the dark and hot. Blessed Be".Not knowing what to expect she hid behind a tall pine tree and gave herself a pretty hefty.....upper. As instructed, Taryn offers The Goddess of Fire the pendant in trade to be blindfolded. The Goddess guides Taryn down a short path where she can feel the heat of fire burn warm against her face. Drums, Louder, She reaches for the Goddesses hand but she is gone. Taryn, the heat, the drums, the dark are left alone. She feels the presence of shadows, almost surrounding her. Her clothes are removed by teeth and long fingers. The drum bangs on, now into a rhythm, music and Taryn? No problem there. She tightened her own blindfold, felt for how close she was to the fire and began to swing her slim hips to the giant drum. The beat can be heard from Detroit. Embers bounce on and off of her vulnerable bare body. Just tiny little sparks of heated pleasure. Drums, smoke, shadows. Taryn, her body pulsates as it begins to glisten with sweat. The beat carries on now matching her heartbeat a pounding yet a swirl of a beat, like the bell ringer going on in her head. She realizes she can't stop dancing, swaying her hips, that now seem to be taken control by such a fiery force. She's gently laid down flat on her back. Embers, smoke, the beat, smoke wraps its lingering fingers around both of her ankles. Raises and widens them. The embers. Smoke, shadows, Taryn. She's breathing deeply while embers skip on and off her aroused nipples, a playground for many in the past. A hot and moist combination tastes her. Front to back, up one side, down the other. She breathes deeper, almost out of breath, the beat, smoke, embers, and Taryn. The tasting travels further back on her. Her backside is lifted gently and ankles spread wider. Now burning hot and moisture rapidly tastes her. The beat, she howls out loud, hot and moist. Hotter, she squirms, Wider, Hotter, Deeper, Heart pounding. Taryn arches her back as if possessed. She throws her head back and lets out a cry of pure ecstasy. Her own moistened reaction puts out the fire. Dark, no beat, silence, smoke, she sits up and feels her pendant round her neck. Taryn just made love to fire.

# The Elements Part 3, Water

*Water is cleansing........*

## Water

Taryn awakes to an owl screeching above her head high in a tree. She realizes she is still stark naked on a bed of ashes. That toned body is smeared with ashes and soot. Hair tussled and mind hung over. She quickly dresses back into holy jeans, black baby tee, and hoodie. She grabs her purse and takes off past the sign that says Next Encampment: Clothing Optional. Taryn exhaled a sigh of relief when she saw large waterfall cascading down three different cliffs. Smaller waterfalls surround them like children. A hot springs borders the cool lake at the bottom. "Thank you," she whispers.

She drops her smoked filled clothing, pulls her hair into a messy pony tail and starts the 20 foot tall hike to the top of the highest cliff. She walks to the edge of the cliff so far her toes are losing to gravity. Abruptly, she hears people. Men, women, screaming.

"Go for it Taryn! Jump! Jump! You got this girl! Come on so we can get to happy hour!!!! Go! Go Taryn! JUMP!"

She takes in a deep breath, closed her eyes, and took the leap of a lifetime. Chanting and cheering are getting louder and louder. But right before she meets the cool connection with the water she remembers, she didn't read the instructions. She plummets deep into the light greenish/bluish water and quickly shoots straight up and out of the water. She wipes her hair from her face and tries to focus on.....where did everyone go? Bewildered, she swam to one of the smaller waterfall. They looked like natural showers. She climbed the mini rocks to get to the natural shower. She lets the lukewarm water fall from the hue of her hair down her soft and toned back peppered with curious tattoos. She lets her hair fall free to get it clean as well. The water flows down past her shoulders, beautiful breasts and belly button. Suddenly, she heard voices coming from all around her,
"Taryn, come on! Let's go! Hurry up! What are you doing? Let's go already!!"
But nobody was there to be found. Just her and the water, she scurried over to a rock that had dry and fresh grey sweatpants and sweatshirt........and instructions. Well actually a letter.

Taryn,
Congratulations! You have successfully completed The Mount Monique Replenishing Retreat! We always leave the last instructions out and away from your reach to see just how far you were willing to cleanse yourself. Taryn, you made love to the moon and danced the forbidden dance with fire and cleansed yourself within the waterfalls. I'm sure you are wondering whose voices were those back at the waterfall. Those voices were actually from your heart. People's hearts you've collected if you will. We all know whoever has a Taryn experience, they belong to you. A reminder of just how many hearts you've stolen. They were just giving the love back. Great job and we'll see you next year.

Sincerely,

Mount Monique Replenishing Retreat Organization

# *Club Heaven*

## ***Heaven don't look like this........***

The line to get into Club Heaven was down the block and around the corner. It was Saturday night and that meant Taryn was the featured act. Once inside, you walk the long hallway which is wall to wall and ceiling to floor mirrors.  Intriguing. You enter a 10 x 20 audience sitting area. It fills quickly. Quiet whispering woman sit patiently. Men rush towards the red curtained round stage untying their ties and pulling out huge bundles of ten, twenty, fifty, and hundred dollar bills. Once the audience is full, the lights go pitch dark and the theater comes to a halt .Total Silence. The MC dressed in a black coattail, red tie, black top hat, and a cane comes from behind the red velvet curtain.

"Ladies and gentleman, please help me welcome our very own,
*"TTTTAAAARRRRRYYYYNNNNN!!!!!"*

The curtain pulls opens as the MC scooted with it to get out of the way. Taryn's set song is Celine Dion and R. Kelly's "I'm your Angel". Simultaneously the curtain pulls and the song fills the room with such bass, it would grab you by the throat and squeeze. But there laid Taryn's lifeless body right there on stage. Random fans ran full speed and hopped up on the stage for their fallen angel was sprawled on the floor. Music stopped. Woman ran out of the building screaming. Even other acts ran to her aide. The whole stage area is pitch black except for one small light bulb. So acts can see where they were going between shows.  Under that dim light, Taryn revealed her pale white skin, blushing cheeks, and rose red lipstick. Suddenly she opens those big brown eyes, winks with a smirk just as she is hoisted so high up into the air. The music began. Everyone looks up in awe (and beads of sweat coming down their head!) They watched with mouths wide open as she ascended to the club's stage.
"Welcome to Club Heaven", whispered the DJ.

The music hits her and the routine is off to a fantastic start. She slowly walks from backstage to upstage with three chairs. It's time to pick 3 suitors. She struts herself down the steps in white lacey panties, bra and 8' tall angel wings.

Hair flows and then falls within her cleavage when she looks down at suitor #1. Bless his dorky little heart she says to herself as she takes him by the collar, gives him a huge lipstick kiss on his cheek and leads him back up onto stage and to the first empty chair.

She gestures two more from the audience to go find a chair up on stage. Men are already whooping and hollering. Jumping up and down hoping she'd pick him. She struts back up onto the stage. She walks across the stage back and forth in front of her tools. She points to the dj and then turned and points at the light crew. Room goes black and the music stops. Taryn straddles the dorky man and leans back so her hair barely kisses the floor. She motions towards the dj and then the light crew. The music comes back but only in acapella. And then the light crew blasts a spotlight on her so bright people had to look away for a second. Men are throwing

money every which way possible. She sits up and rubs against him and flips her blond hair over her head and his. She winks and he puts a fifty dollar bill in her garter.
Suitor #1 is a business owner of some sort, dark blue suit with matching tie.

Men are screaming whooping and hollering, tossing money all over the stage. This time Taryn stands behind the well-dressed fellow. She snaps twice and the same thing happens. No music. Lights down. She snaps her instructions again. The music comes back as its original track but still only one spotlight. This time Taryn slowly manages to put her long leg and tiny foot over his shoulder right at his crouching tiger. He rubs his hand up and down her soft subtle leg. Even leans over and kissed her thigh. She unties his tie and puts it round her own neck. He lightly throws multiple hundred dollar bills at her feet.

Next but not least, another direction is given, ALL, lights out. The first two "customers" are escorted off stage. A thin stage wide white screen slowly rolls down from the ceiling to the stage. A spotlight from behind the stage illuminates just shadows.  Men's shadows throwing money onto the stage is just great scenery.

Last Taryn gives the dj one more signal and with the light crew placing that spotlight BEHIND the screen is not much but will come out smooth if executed properly. Music began acapella and the spotlight actually captures Taryn being benched pressed from behind the white screen by her third beau.  He shreds the screen with his heavy boot and steps through revealing her third beau is a body builder! She rests her hand against her head pretending to yawn. The crowd goes wild and roaring ENCORE!!!!!! Red velvet curtain goes to close right before she blows a kiss and glitter falls from above.

The plump MC appears from the side of the stage.
"Thank you ladies and gents for coming out! Was that not a show or what? Come back and see us again next Saturday. Our very own Taryn shall give us another breathtaking little ditty! Have a great night and remember, Heaven Must Be Missing An Angel!"

# *The Blonde*

### Reflection........

**T**aryn is driving home The Watering Hole one warm and quiet night. She opens the sunroof as she rides the boulevard. All was a calm night for the exception of.....her passenger.
Earlier that evening.....

A buxom blonde was quite intoxicated and heavily infatuated with Taryn all evening. Taryn goes to the powder room, there she stood. Taryn competes to catch a Jell-O shot, the blonde is right next to her. Taryn is dancing with a good looking guy and the blonde; once again, she's right there. Always willing to accept the love, Taryn decides not to show distress. She notices the blonde is at the bar taking shots of tequila back to back. She's falling out of her one size too small purple tube top. Her mascara is running and her lipstick is smeared. While dancing with a few girlfriends, Taryn looks up just in time to see her newest admirer is coming her way. She is staggering, tripping over her own feet, and waving her arms wildly in the air. Taryn takes her beautiful disaster by both hands and pulls her into her own inner space. She looks up and over her shoulder towards the dj booth. She makes eye contact with the dj and simply winks. The dj nods and the lights dim to a low purple light and a sensual tempo beat slows down the dance floor to more or less, a gentle groove. Taryn places her forehead to the blonde's forehead, still holding both of her hands. If anyone can tame this creature, it's Taryn. The two women slowly dance side to side, their eyes are closed. The slow jam ends and regular lights brighten the building signaling the end of another eventful night at The Watering Hole. Worried her new friend may have trouble getting home safely, Taryn offers her to go home with her for the night. Of course the offer was received with screams and shrieks of joy.

During the ride to her apartment, Taryn learns that her new companion gets very emotional once alcohol settles into her system. Within a simple fifteen minute drive, she had cried, laughed, passed out, smoked four cigarettes, and cursed her ex-boyfriend for sleeping with her sister. They arrive at Taryn's apartment shortly after. After locking the door behind her, Taryn shows the blonde where the bathroom is and offers her t-shirt to change into. As her guests changes in the bathroom, Taryn also changes into a black nightgown. She meets her guest in the hallway and shows her to the guest room. After getting her settled in, Taryn returns to her bedroom and lies across the bed, exhausted. Suddenly she hears a knock at her bedroom door. She sits up straight as the blonde opens the door, enters, closes it behind her, and stand there with a sheepish look on her face. Taryn pats the space next to her on her bed. Her guest joins her and lays her head on Taryn's lap. Taryn softly rubs her back as she drifts off to a sweet slumber.

Taryn must have laid back and dozed off for a while. She opens her eyes to a warm and moist sensation between her legs. Her houseguest is caressing Taryn's sugar walls with her tongue. She gently squeezes her supple breasts. Taryn arches her back grips the white satin sheets. Her thighs begin to quiver and goosebumps arise around her aldols. She gently grabs the hair of her pleaser and cries out sealing her climax.

Taryn places her left hand on the mane of the blonde tendrils as they freely fall on and off of her toned stomach. And lets the other arm fall to the opposite side of the bed. She slowly opens her eyes and examines the precious picturesque image of a beautiful and naked blonde resting her head on Taryn's nude stomach in her mirrored ceiling. Petting her pawn in her game of lust. Then a sudden quick pinch. Suddenly she turns to her right just in time to see Jay fall back into the shadows and the romps and swirls immediately follow.

# Fraternity Penford

*Taryn volunteers to mother hen the popular frat house at her alma mater........*

Our dearest Taryn,

We are formally inviting you back to your great alma mater MPU to mother hen the university's infamous Fraternity Penford. A fraternity known to throw the best parties, practice the utmost respectable rituals is the number one fraternity to participate in charities and fundraisers. All "A" honor roll. Quite a groomed Dapper Dan type group of guys, well mannered, respects their elders, and emulates the Greek Gods. They are all aspiring doctors, lawyers, and business owners. These boys are our "leaders of tomorrow" we hope you accept this request we look forward to your arrival."

Taryn smirks and drops the invitation down to her glass coffee table.
"And they are all total horn dogs behind closed doors, nasty bastards."
But of course she's going to do it.....it'd be good for her....moral.

Taryn dressed in a purple form fitting pant suit, black camisole giving plenty of cleavage (school colors, black and purple) and black heels meets Dean Ross with a firm handshake in front of the Frat Penford house. It was a beautiful warm September afternoon. The guys were quietly mowing the lawn, washing windows, watering flowers, sun tanning in a beach chair in the front yard, and one studying at a picnic table with ear plugs in on the side yard. "Thank you again Taryn for your services. I'm sure the brothers will welcome you with open arms," says Dean Ross wiping his sweating forehead with a handkerchief. "Pleasure's all mine Dean Ross. The brothers are safe with me," she replied She watched him walk the same waddle of a walk away. The man was overweight when she was student. Once he was well out of sight, she pivoted on her heels towards the house. She walked four steps through the white picket fence and then to the middle of the walkway, paused and crossed her arms. She walked four steps to the middle of the walkway, paused, and crossed her arms. "Alright fellas, Ross is gone so you can cut the charade," she said. All of a sudden, she heard an outburst of,

"Whoo-hoo!!! She's here!"

"Dude! She's really here!"

Seriously bro! She's here?"

As Taryn enters the Fraternity Penford front door, she is followed by:

**Joshua,**
Major: Business Law
Vice: Alcohol

**Derek,**
Major: Nuclear Physics
Vice: Gambling

**Brandon,**
Vice: Substance intake
Major: Universal Medicine

**Zack,** "the Quarterback"
Major: Sports journalism (promising NFL draft candidate)
Vice: Women
She settles on the sectional couch that sits in the middle of the living room. The students line up in front of her. She takes her blazer off and tosses it halfway over the back of the couch then stands and sensually paces back and forth in front of the students.

"Rules," she said quietly.
The lineup suddenly quits fidgeting. They stand tall as if in boot camp.

They begin in unison,

**1.** For the next three months Taryn is in charge. Respect and trust her authority.
**2.** We must uphold our studies and extracurricular activities as did our Greek gods.
**3.** As Penford men, we have a responsibility to be true to ourselves, mind, body, and soul. Taryn is walking around the living room closing windows. She closes and locks the front door. Then turns and quietly asks,

"And?"
With a touch of mischief in their voice, her lineup replies,
"What happens in this house stays in this house." The brothers relax slap high fives and cheer, "Penford, Penford, Penford!"
During the next three months Taryn assists the frat house in everyday living activities such as picking up jerseys and letterman jackets from the dry cleaner's, proofreading thesis papers, picking up empty pizza boxes from each bedroom, folding laundry, and washing dishes. She also ran curb patrol every Saturday night, fished bongs and thongs out of the swimming pool out back, and snapping homecoming pictures. Taryn watches their every move and sees they are truly good guys. She decides to treat the brothers.....after midterms.
It's a blistering cold December Thursday evening. The campus is preparing to shut down for the winter holiday break. All midterms or finals are completed and submitted. Students are hustling to finish last minute Christmas shopping and pack their dorm rooms before heading back home for the holidays. After the 47th Annual Penford Fraternity Paintball Tournament, the brothers file back into the frat house. Not one of them has any idea what's waiting for them once the door closes. As they begin to peel off their coats, hats, and backpacks, all of their cell phones light up, vibrate, and sound off at the same time. They've all received a text message from Taryn that reads:

My dearest men of Penford Fraternity,
I trust you are the undefeated champions of the paintball tournament yet again!!!Well, I wanted to let you know that I am so proud of all of you this semester. You worked so hard on your studies and welcoming new pledges. You've made me so proud to be your mother hen once again. I've left a little something for each of you in your bedrooms.
Remember,
"What happens in this house stays in this house." I expect great things.
Yours forever,
"T"
Go Penford!

The brothers take off down the hallway and each stop in front of their own bedroom doors. They are all breathing heavily as they turn and look at one another. Josh puts his hand on his door knob first. He holds his breath and turns it open. He steps inside and closes the door behind him. After he flips the light switch, he's greeted by a woman dressed in all black lingerie and a black bow tie. She is standing behind a mini bar on the left side of his bedroom. She is wiping down an already sparkling tumbler with a bright white towel. He walks closer and takes a seat at the lone bar stool across from his barmaid. He notices the wall behind her is stocked full with a bountiful display of different types of gin, whiskey, brandy, tequila, and rum. He gulps as his barmaid slides an empty sparkling shot glass across the bar towards him.

"What's your poison?" she asks with a wink.

Derek enters his room next. Before he could flip the light switch on, he can hear coins collecting in the dark. After he flips the switch, he quickly learns the light switch not only operated the simple three way bulb that usually lights his bedroom, but that night, yes, that night it illuminated the room with a bright slot machine with a long golden handle. A long craps table took the place of his bed. The right wall was transformed into a giant roulette wheel. The left wall was now a ceiling to floor Keno screen. A woman dressed as a Las Vegas showgirl with brilliant purple feathers and a beautiful smile greeted him with a silver tray filled with a stack of assorted dollar bills, poker chips, a pair of red dice, and a Cuban cigar. With very little hesitation, Derek takes one small step towards his server and her tray and slowly reaches for the red dice and poker chips. He takes the stack of cash and slipped it into his back pocket. Finally, he takes the cigar and runs it under his nose, inhaling the sweet smell. He makes his way to the end of the craps table and wipes the sweat from his forehead. His server steps next to him and states, "Good luck."

It is Brandon's turn to enter his bedroom. He takes a deep breath and turns the knob. Once inside, he looks around the room, left to right. All is dark and quiet. He reaches for the light switch but the flick of a lighter catches his eye instead. He follows the small flame to a loveseat in the middle of the room. It has a black, red, and green afghan slung over the back of it. A rectangle glass coffee table sits in front of the loveseat and a thirteen inch flat screen television is found against the wall. A lonesome white candle sits on the top right corner of the coffee table. As Brandon gets closer to the candle lit corner, he notices the walls are covered in posters of Bob Marley, Buddha, and psychedelic peace signs. He sits on the loveseat and discovers some items lined up on the table. There laid different color and size pipes, scale, grinder, tweezers, lighter, rolling papers credit card , bottle of water, aluminum foil, straws, silver spoon, alcohol swabs, orange caps, and cotton balls. Also quarter sized plastic packages full of many different treats. As he studies the content on the table in front of him, his heart starts to race. Suddenly another flick of a lighter breaks his concentration. It came from the left side of the loveseat.

She's wearing ripped jeans, purple tye-dye tank top with a peace sign on the front, and blonde dread locks with rainbow beads threaded through them.
She sits up, hands him a joint, and asks,

"Hey bro, want a hit?"

Finally Zack the Quarterback enters his bedroom. Once inside, he flips the light switch. His eyes dart towards his bed. There laid three beautiful women wrapped up in football jerseys with his number (33) on the back.  Each had black stiletto heels on. One was a red head heavily decorated with tattoos, another was a blonde, her hair pulled up in a tight pony tail with rose red blushed cheeks, and last but never least, a brunette with thick thighs. She blows him a kiss. He stands still with his mouth opened wide.  Two more women come from behind him and undress him down to his boxer briefs. An electric sign that flashes bright fluorescent red says, Girls! Girls! Girls! flashes above his bed. Zack The Quarterback lies on his back as he watches all five women undress one another. The red head steps forward from the rest of the women. She walks right to the edge of the bed. Then climbs up onto the bed and slowly crawls between Zack The Quarterback's legs. She stops just shy of her cleavage brushing against the bulge in his boxer briefs.

She looks dead into his eyes and whispers "Are you ready?"

# *Yes Mr. Adams*

## *Power....at first........*

Receptionist: "You are to meet Mr. Adams at 433 Prospect Place tomorrow 8 am sharp. Please dress appropriately. Mr. Adam's will be giving you directions on what to do, any questions?" Taryn: "No I got it. Thank you."

The next day Taryn is in Mr. Adams lobby. Fish tanks and plants decorate the spacious room. He comes out of his office dressed in a slight grey suite with a purple tie and matching handkerchief, salt and peppered low haircut chiseled hands.

"Phyllis, has the new temp arrived yet?" Phyllis gestured towards Taryn who was in a lilac purple suit jacket and mini skirt with simple black heels. She's sitting with her legs crossed like Fatal Attraction. She was reading the latest issue of Time Magazine. He walks over to her. Their eye contact is fierce. One hand is in his left pocket. He offers her the other chiseled hand. "Hello. You must be Taryn. I am Winston Q. Adams. Welcome aboard.
"

As Mr. Adams shows her his office by the small of her back, he adds, "Phyllis, take a two hour lunch. You deserve it. Just lock up on your way out. Thanks." Rolling her eyes, Phyllis grabs her purse and keys and locks the door from the outside. He went to go secure his office door and when he comes back into his office he finds her in his Corinthian leather chair and she spins around with those long legs kicked up and crossed on his desk.

Untying his tie, Mr. Adams explained, "I am your supervisor. You are my subordinate. "Taryn stands straight up and replies, as he walks over behind her, "Anything for you Mr. Adams!"
As he inhales from her ear lobe and says, "You even smell rich. I hope you are just as moist. Bend over."

She follows directions and wipes off the whole desk with one swift sweep of her arm, stapler, photos, files, pen cup, sticky notes, everything goes flying.

"Lift your skirt," he says. She abides swiftly. He unzips his pants.

"Hold on, wait," he exclaims. I want to examine your assets."

He steps back and looks at her backside. The adventure ends just as it began.
"Hold on," he repeated breathlessly as he pounds it into her.

She lets out a little whimper but continues to hold on to his freshly polished mahogany desk. His grunting turns her on. Harder pounding continues. He's ready to give his finale.

"Yeah! Yeah! Yeah!" he pulls on her hair as he empties out in her.

Taryn pulls her lavender lace underwear up and pulls her skirt down and grabs her purse. She was already in the elevator with the doors half closing when Mr. Adams barely catches her frantically pulling his pants up.

 Out of breath he exclaims, "I'll call you."

Taryn replies, No you won't, "Mr. 44 seconds"!!!

# T&T



## <u>Tabitha</u>

T

he stretch limo transports its two passengers who ride quietly and content. Traveling towards the north side of the railroad tracks, the limo slowly approached the Bella Spencer Center where the annual Governor's Ball is being held. The limo parks at the bottom of the red carpeted stairs that lead up to the grand soiree. A tall three piece suit exits the limo, turns around, and extends a long and strong arm with a diamond studded cuff linked hand into the limo. A lovely, soft, and elegant hand took his firm offer slowly. A long satin cream colored elbow length glove took the diamond studded cuff link hand and stood tall and slender from the limo. She's wearing a floor satin strapless cream colored gown with matching gloves. A generous size princess cut white diamond ring accent her left gloved index finger, a matching pearl calla lily pendant and diamond stud earrings complete her jewelry ensemble. They slowly climb the sixteen red carpeted staircase surrounded by media snapping pictures with bright flashes capturing the elegant couple.  They reach the top with glass doors reaching high into the sky with platinum handles. They are met by the governor himself. He reaches and shake's her beau's hand and gently kisses her hand. As he lets go of her small hand go he whispers," Enchante." She coyly smiles and nods her head. An attendant opens the door, bows his head, and gestures for them to enter.

# <u>Taryn</u>

The black Charger burns rubber as it crosses the railroad tracks facing the south side of town. The sports car spins into a parking spot ending in a puff of exhaust. Before he could get out of the car and open the door for his lovely lady date, Taryn had already spilled out of the passenger seat holding a bottle of Patron in one hand and slamming the car door with the other hand. She just about trips over the heel of her own thigh high boot's when her guy catches her just in the nick of time. He inhales her combination scent of Obsession perfume behind her ear, the scent of pure leather of her jacket, and the Patron from her breath. They head across the parking lot towards "The Watering Hole." The bar/dance club usually frequents at, he catches her by her firm and fit ass clothed with a matching black mini skirt. They stumble to the end of the line. She leans against the brick wall, wraps her arms around his neck and kisses him wildly yet passionately at the same time. The wall behind her rumbles with the bass of the Dj spinning a new record. Nobody else in line pays attention to the drunken couple making out. They finally reach the door where a seven foot 280 pound man greets Taryn with a big smile. Picks her up and spins her around. Slowly puts her down and says,

**"T. Where you been at baby doll? Damn you look good!"**
She curtsies. He gestures for her to go inside. He stops her date in mid stride with one hand. Then pats him down. Taryn yelled over the festivities," He's cool Bear! Come on!"
Bouncer Bear still asks him for identification and charged him full cover charge.

# <u>Tabitha</u>

Bankers, investors, businessman, accountants, and attorneys all shake her beau's hand or pats him on the back congratulating him on closing the big Miller account earlier that week. Tabitha elegantly removed a fluke of champagne from a passing tray and nods her head to those who acknowledge her presence first. Her beau appears and nudges her along by one hand at the middle of her back. He feels her skin. She feels so warm, honest, and comfortable. Toned and tanned with a darker brunette colored hair pinned up with just a few tendrils cascading down her subtle back. After having small and meaningless conversations with the other colleague's wives she thought her head would split in half.

"I think I'm changing tanners. I'm mean look at me. Total polar pale."

"Well, you know the country club's personal tennis instructor, Blain? Well.... It's true......it does curve to the right."

"Umm, Well I got confirmation Robert is sleeping with his secretary Sandra. He told me earlier on the phone that he couldn't have lunch. That he was going over briefs. So, I brought him a picnic surprise. Walked in. Oh yeah. He was going over briefs. He was wearing her purple lace thong and a gag in his mouth. And she was totally naked but wearing his tie, spanking him with a whip." She takes a giant gulp of her champagne.

Another asked, "Is there lipstick on my teeth?"

At 8pm sharp A Matrade with an uncanny resemblance to Alfred Hitchcock enters the lobby with a solemn expression, lifts an antique bell and rang it three times.

"Dinner will be served in approximately 10 minutes." Then a line of what looked like a line of penguins with trays turned out to be a line of servers with bright white and starched shirts and crisp black bow ties follow the matrade and began serving mostly champagne and assorted mixed drinks Appetizers began as an extra-large shrimp cocktail, oyster stew, rare ribeye cutlets, twice baked potatoes, and a chocolate flambé. The crowd claps their hands when the flambé is served but the crowd quietly just claps and shows no emotion.

# <u>Taryn</u>

Once inside, Taryn is sucked right into the dance floor. A beat hits the speakers and everyone seemed to move to it as if choreographed. Hands reach out just to touch and slap her high five. Exchange daps. She's trying to get her date to come out to the dance floor. A wallflower wonderful, Oh well! Her attention is deterred to someone either pinching or slapping her ass.. Fingers running through her full head of big curls. The black halter top she is sporting is slick and sharp. A slim blonde bartender with red highlights and tight holy jeans screams, "FORE!!!!!!!!!!!!!!!!!!!! " Everyone's heads turn towards her and all arms reach high into the sky. Then she adds medium sized Jell-O shots into an adult size sling shot strung from all over corners of the wraparound bar. She pulls back and shoots her artillery into the crowd. Guys dodge forward with their baseball caps. Women open their shirts in hope to catch one in their cleavage. Some partiers just open their mouths and hope to just catch one in their mouths. Taryn is on top of Bouncer Bear's shoulders and catches one straight into her mouth. She gives the "field goal "signal and everyone cheers and scream, "TARYN! TARYN! TARYN! Once back on the floor, she slaps a couple more high fives. Gets dipped and kissed by a random but handsome fellow. She finally gets to the bar and grabs a handful of cashews, peanuts, and maraschino cherries as snacks. Taryn observes the scenery. "Her club", how proud of the work she's put into becoming a well-known regular. Two twenty somethings approached Taryn with screeches and hugs. She smiles at them hugs them back at the same time. Bartender bellows," FORE!!!!!!!!!!!!!!!!!!!!!!!! "This time Taryn ducks and laughs. She stood up and thought it was time to do a hair and makeup check. So she headed to the lady's room. As she walked into the lady's room, she pulled out what looked like a small black pouch. As she opened the pouch, her phone rang. Whatever was in that pouch had to wait!

# Tabitha

"Hey T. It's Tabby. Listen. Can we switch tonight? This ball is such a sleeper. I want to be in your world. Do what you do. Well, maybe not everything. But you know what I mean? Please?"

# Taryn

" Well. Well. Well. If it isn't my haughty taughty well to do cousin Tabitha. Tell me Tabby. How are things on The Hills?" replied Taryn teasingly. Taryn quietly thought to herself as she reapplied a thick layer of mascara. *Well, it is pretty dry out here anyway*." Alright, Alright, Alright, meet me at my place in fifteen."

# Tabitha

" Monroe, to T's place, please" asked Tabitha to her limo driver. Once at Taryn's apartment complex parking lot, Tabitha gets out of her limo, closes the door, leaned against it, and lights a cigarette.

# Taryn

Taryn screams into a parking spot of her apartment building. Instantly sees her cousin taking a drag from a cigarette in a gorgeous cream evening gown.
"Since when did you start smoking?" asked her cousin.

# Tabitha

"There are a lot of things people don't know about me, cuz! Oh, can I wear your leather coat? It always feels so good!"

# Taryn

"Huh, I bet, Taryn replied. Alright, let's get this party started right."
Walking up the stairs leading to Taryn's apartment, Taryn replies, only if I can get your "iced" out neck choker!

# Tabitha

" Ok, Tabitha sighed. Quick instructions: The Governor's Ball is strictly black tie. You must wear a long evening gown. Hair must be pinned up.

# Taryn

As Tabitha is babbling, Taryn has already pinned her hair up, slipped into a black evening gown exposing "that thigh", with lace sleeves, and black high heels. Iced diamond neck choker clasped and accents the diamond ankle bracelet and diamond earrings.

# Tabitha

Tabitha is in one of Taryn's wardrobe rooms filing through miniskirts, halter tops, pant suits, and form fitting cocktail dresses. She chooses a black cocktail dress. Unpins her brunette hair letting it breathe and cascade down her back. Black eyeliner, black mascara, candy apple lipstick is applied and the leather jacket completes the look.

The cousins meet in the hallway almost in a perfect reflection of each other.

# Taryn

"Let's do this," says Taryn. She looks her cousin up and down making sure everything is on point. She unzips her jacket her Cousin Tabitha is wearing just enough to reveal the perfect cleavage. She steps back and exclaims, "There!"

## Tabitha

As thigh high boots and black high heel shoes clamber down the three flights of stairs, the girls had no idea what the night had in store for them.
"T! She screams. Keys!"

## Taryn

"In the front pocket, have fun and call me if you need me!" screamed Taryn over her shoulder as Monroe opens the door and Taryn eases into the limo.

## Tabitha

As she watched her limo drive Taryn towards the other side of the railroad tracks, she playfully tossed the keys to the Charger into the air and catches them. She entered the diver seat of the Charger, started the engine just as Prince was singing, "Little Red Corvette."

## Taryn

Taryn arrives at the Governor's Ball almost as it was coming to an end.
"Wait here, Monroe," she ordered. "Yes ma'am," he replied as he let her out and closes the door gently behind her and stands there diligently awaiting his passenger.
She swallows hard wondering if she put the neck choker on a

little too tight. She slowly climbs the sixteen red carpeted steps and is met by that same diamond cuff linked beau. She looks up with eyes sparkling and glistening due to all of the media's flashing going stark raving mad over her unexpected cameo. Her ears are buzzing due to all of the whispering of the party goers leaving the Bella Spencer Center because she had arrived and graced them with her presence. She reaches for his firm hand. He bends to kiss it but she caught his eyes sneaking a peak of her heavenly cleavage. Just then the Governor pushes the staring beau to the side and gently kisses her hand and adds," Enchante." She smiles coyly and blushes.

# Tabitha

Tabitha pulls into the parking lot of "The Watering Hole." She lights a cigarette and struts towards the building. She's free for one night. Don't blow it. She walks to the front of the building as many drunk and loud patrons are stumbling out and whisper something into Bouncer Bear's ear. He takes her by one hand and slowly spins her around like a ballerina twice looking her up and down.

"Yup, you are definitely related to "T". Go on in there before I shut it down."

He gestures for her to enter and she did with almost a giddy skip. He watches her enter thinking,

"Good God." And shakes his head.
Inside she hears," LAST CALL!!!!!" over the speakers. But she jumps right onto the dance floor and cuts loose. Random guys hand her drinks. Bottom's up was her attitude. She soaked up the strobe light by spinning around, random bodies rubbing against each other as the dj drops a mind boggling bass blowing record as his finale. The crowd goes mad. Then the lights come on. The music stops. Rowdy frat

boys head to after parties. Middle aged women seem unsatisfied and searching for their car keys in their purses. Coat check line is ridiculous.  Drunken men with absolutely no game are trying to collect phone numbers from annoyed pretty girls. Tabitha's world is spinning. She just recently learned not to mix tequila and spiced rum. Outside, leaned against the cool brick wall of the club, she can't decide to vomit or just keel over and die. Then the black Charger came screaming right up next to her.

# <u>Taryn</u>

As Taryn and her beau re-enter the limo together, he whispers something into her small ear. She looks around as if someone heard him. He nudged her back softly as she entered and sat quietly like a lady. He entered from the other side and as he got comfortable he pushed a light on the door that dimmed all light around them. He picks up the phone and says," Monroe, back to Taryn's, the long way old sport!" He hung up the phone and she can see his shadow move quickly towards her face kissing her wildly in the pure dark back of the limo and the couple become quite hot and heavy. She's holding his head by the back of his ears. One of his hands has a hold of "that thigh ". The other barely touched the dimmer light switch. He let go of "that thigh "and slowly and slightly lit the limo. He kissed her luscious lips. His masculine arms unzip the zipper in the back of her satin and lace black dress. Kisses her shoulders, he pulls the dress down past her fantastic breasts with a strapless black demy bra past her oval naval. Then past her black lacey thong underwear.

" Oh my God," he said as he caresses her breasts. "Leave your heels on," he whispers.

He unravels his bowtie. She rips his crisp white shirt and buttons fly everywhere. His flawless chest is breathing heavily against hers. He begins to feel the inside of her arms. Where her arm and elbow meet, tapping them, looking at them with such intensity, *no way,* she thought.

He wrapped her arm with his tie. She watches as he feels her arm, sticks, infiltrates, pulls back, bull's-eye, push, untie tie, and her eyes roll to the back of her head. He hits himself quickly then dims the light again to total darkness. He pulls down her underwear and shoves them into his mouth and then places her legs over his shoulders. She whimpers and thank God it's a stretch limo.

# Tabitha

"Get in," he said. It was the goatee with short shiny curly hair. Confused, Tabitha stuttered, "But this. I mean. Umm. This is my cousin's car, Taryn."

"Yes this is T's ride, he said. She gave me an extra set for safe keeping and emergencies. She also asked me to look after you tonight."

Teeth clattering, he asked, "Now can we please go. It's freezing out here."

Tabitha walks right up to her protector and lays a fat and wet one right on his sharp chiseled lips. She pulled away and let him help her into the front seat. Once he's got her in safe, he jogs around the front of the car and hops into the driver side. As he sits, Tabitha reached to make out with him. As he put the car into drive, her head disappears down his front side. Off to a great start.

Once parked in Taryn's parking lot, it is pouring a cool and crisp rain and there low and behold is Tabitha lying on her back on the warm hood of Taryn's Charger. Her legs spread wide as the curly haired goatee gives her the business. Her black dress is up over her cool and erect breasts. As he's going for the gold, he's moaning, she's screaming, she grabs his shoulders, and in unison they both let out a cry of ecstasy. The rain is pounding on the earth as he pounds in on her. He bottoms out and makes a hefty deposit into her sugar walls. He leans his head on her breast as he tries to catch his breath. But she quickly gets up, pushes him away, and gets in the car.

"I can't find my underwear! And Taryn's leather jacket! Oh my God! Oh my God!!! If I lose that jacket she'd make sure they wouldn't find my body for six months. Trust! She knows I've been in that jacket in the rain all night. Shit!"

He walks up behind her now bent over inside car. She can feel he is ready for round two.

"Shhhh....he whispered. Your underwear are in my pocket. And the jacket is right here."

This turned her on. He slipped her black cocktail dress down and she lifts her feet to get it off. He zips up her jacket all of the way, grabs her hand and they both run into the apartment building out of the rain, dressed in just her cousin's jacket.

# <u>Taryn</u>

After it seems like hours of clutching the safety handles on the roof of the limo and six toe curling climaxes, Taryn sat up and on the warm and wet limo seat totally out of breath. Her environment is still dark and warm. She reaches around for her underwear all the while trying not to tip over due to the limo was still in motion. As she dresses, she requests,

"Monroe, home please,"

"Of course," he replied

Her beau is lying across the limo seat. Head behind her. Pants still down around his ankles. Both insides of her arms are bruised and swollen. They arrive at Taryn's parking lot shortly afterwards.  Taryn steps out holding her heels in her hand and dress on but only halfway zipped. She closes the limo door and holding up her dress so it does not drag on the gravel. The limo began to slowly move away when the back window rolls down. Her beau appeared still panting like a puppy. He gulps and says, "Tabitha, you are amazing. I want to see you again. You have a body of a Goddess."

Taryn bent over into the warm limo, the smell of sex and treats.

"Baby, Tabitha is a twit in a tiara. I sir, am Taryn. The one and ONLY who rocked your world."
She steps away and taps the trunk of the limo as a sign to leave. It rolls away slowly into the darkness.

# Tabitha

Still drunk, he helps her into the bathroom. She drops the sopping leather jacket to the floor and stumbles into the shower. She hears her suitor enter the bathroom and tinker on the countertop. It's so hot and steamy, she can't see anything.
"When you're done, just put a robe on, ok?" he asked.
She follows instructions. Still steamy, she exits the bathtub and puts on a nearby hanging robe. He takes her arm and rolls up the sleeve. Pokes, infiltrate, pull back, crimson red, then push. He gives himself a treat and unties her robe, lifts one of her legs over his shoulders. He tastes every inch of her promise land. She returns the favor swallowing every drop offered.
He clothes her in comfy fleece pajamas and carries her to bed. Gives her a bell ringer and leaves the apartment locking it behind him.

# Taryn

Taryn didn't see her car so she figured what's his name still has the car. Exhausted, she takes the elevator. Unlocked her apartment and instantly smells her shampoo. Hmm, Tabby must be here. She climbed her spiraling staircase and headed to her bedroom to undress. She turns the light on and Tabitha sits straight up, eyes dilated by light years. "You won't believe what happened tonight!!!" exclaimed Tabitha.
Taryn tossed her shoes to the floor, turned around and motioned for her cousin to finish unzipping her, drops the dress, steps out of it (again for the second time tonight) and

plops back on her large purple bean bag that sits adjacent to her bed. Still in her black demy bra and matching lacey thong, crossing those long legs. Taryn felt she was in a real life Rocky Horror Picture Show scene. She was Columbia and Magenta screaming, **"Tell us about it Janet!!!!"** But she was far from screaming it, just thinking, she was too damn tired to sing. It seemed like Tabitha is over on the bed morphing into Janet Wise. " Touch-a, Touch-a, Touch-a me! I want to feel dirty!!!!!"""" Taryn let her finish her story.
Tabitha asks, "And your night?"
But before Taryn could get off the runway, Tabitha was sleep. Sound, Taryn covers her up.
"Sleep tight Tabby. Sleep tight."

*Slumber Party*

***An Adult Slumber Party........***

"I thought Taryn said she'd be here by now."

"Don't worry. She'll be here. Come on let's finish getting stuff around for her."

The bubbly red headed identical twins Shanna and Shaina rustled around the hotel suite lighting candles, creating playlists on an mp3 player, placing a heart shaped bottle of glittery bubble bath next to the whirlpool, pulling the curtains closed, pouring champagne into three long stem champagne glasses, arranging a bowl of strawberries and storing in the mini refrigerator, placing new batteries and memory cards in three brand new cameras and putting them on the bedside, placing new batteries and memory cards in three brand new cameras and putting them on the bedside, and hanging four sheer black scarves over the headboard. The girls were also instructed to place a medium sized silver platter on the bathroom counter with a cup of water, a box of orange caps, alcohol swabs, a large rubber band type thing and a spoon.

"Why this?" asked Shaina with a very peculiar expression a crossed her face. "I think I heard Taryn say she was a diabetic or something. I don't know," replied Shanna with a shrug.

BUZZZZZZZ!!!! BUZZZZZ!!!!

The twins instantly look at the phone buzzing across the counter.
They both screech,
 "It's her!" They bolt for the phone.

Shaina answers the phone, "Hello?" Hi Taryn! Ok. Uh-huh". She looks at her sister. "Uh-huh. Ok. Bye!" She never takes her eyes off of her sister. With bright and widened green eyes, the opposite sister asks, "Well? What? What'd she say?!"
Her sister answered, "She said she was in the parking lot. We are to be in the hot tub with pink bubbles, champagne, strawberries and one camera and to start drinking."

The twins didn't think twice as they dropped jeans, lacey panties, t-shirts, and bras. Steam and giggling escape from the whirlpool room as Taryn enters the hotel room with Jay in tow. She quickly took off her black suede jacket revealing a rather simple but casual white racer back tank top, low-cut jeans, and matching black suede boots. Tosses the jacket on the bed and asked Jay to close the door and lock it. The sway of her hips matched her next statement,
"We got work to do."

### *Everyone gets treats and presents........*

Taryn stares at herself in a full body mirror admiring her fabulous ensemble, an all red pant suit. The suit coat is tailored with the sleeves cut off, Cleavage forever.  Shoes similar to Dorothy's ruby red slippers, nails painted red with a clear glitter coat.  A simple ponytail tied with a red satin bow with just a little red blush and red lipstick.

She makes her way down the decorated staircase. Fixing the wreaths she thought to herself
A Red Christmas

Once in the dining room, she lights the candles on the dining room table. Taryn then checks the full stockings in the living room that are all embroidered  with names such as Jay, Shanna and Shaina, The Musician, Tabitha, etc., etc.

She peers outside the frosty window just in time to see all of her guests pulling into the long and heated driveway leading up to her large six bedroom four bathroom fully furnished cabin. She grabs a black mink cloak with an oversized hood that was made for her and walks out to the front porch to greet her guests.  She can see her breath as it escapes her perky red lips. She smiles her pearly white smile and waves and jumps up and down like a cheerleader as each guest exits their vehicles, you can hear car alarms setting.  As they hold each other to ward off the cold weather. Their free arms are jam packed with poinsettias, wreaths, purple gift bags, small, medium, and large brightly wrapped boxes, crock pots, and appetizer trays. Silly Santa hats and antler ear hats cover her beloved's cold heads. She impatiently opens her arms and hands to welcome with warm hugs as they reach the top of the stairs. First to arrive," Tabby!!! Merry Christmas!" screeched Taryn.

"Merry Christmas, T, giggled Tabitha and embraced her cousin. You look sensational."
Taryn replies, "Girl, please. Get inside. It's cold. I love you. Now go."

Tabitha followed directions in a 50's style green flare dress with red heels. Hair down with holly pinned to the left side of her head.

Next the Irish Twins, Shanna and Shaina carefully run up the stairs hand in hand each with a perfectly squared gift box tucked under their alternate arm. At the same time, each twin places their box on the steps and jump in Taryn's arms like a long lost big sister. She holds both of her young girls tight. One sniffles. The other tried to hold it in.

"Shh", replied Taryn. You're here now. I'm here. Tonight, we get stupid. She giggles. Ok?"
She pulls them away and kisses their tears. Now go inside. Eat snacks BEFORE you hit the bar!" she yelled after them as they grabbed their gifts and run full force through the door. A man clears his throat which makes Taryn turn around quickly.

"Monroe, she said quietly. Thank you so much for coming."
She kisses him on his cold ear.
"I wouldn't miss it for the world, Miss Taryn, replied Monroe. You never treated me like a
domestic.  You treated me like a human. And for that, I protected you whenever I escorted you."
 He bows his head slightly and hands her a bracelet size gift wrapped box from Jared.
"Merry Christmas, Miss Taryn."

 In tears, Taryn slowly takes the gift and tucks it into a hidden pocket of her cloak.
"Merry Christmas, Monroe. They embrace warmly. Now go inside. It's freezing."
Through chattering teeth, he replies,
"Yes ma'am," and continues on into the cabin.

Next was good old Jay quickly walking up the stairs fussing at not one but two beautifully
tanned, blue eyed, Ken doll like twins wearing matching pea coats and khaki pants. Jay kisses
Taryn on the cheek. "Merry Christmas, my heart, we would have been here but somebody
wanted to play Mr. GPS!"

As he glares at one of the Ken dolls. Taryn rolls her eyes.
"Alright, Alright girls, Inside, Go." Both Ken dolls stumble up the stairs then each kiss Taryn on
each cheek she extends her arms and each kiss the inside of her arms.
 "Merry Christmas" they say in unison.

"Well alright, she replied with a giggle". Now go on inside for appetizers and drinks."
Jay acknowledges with a smile and a wink as he nudges them along.
"Get in there you three, there had to be 2, dear God please help me! As they get closer to the
door, Jay yells inside," Bartender! Give me a double of anything, please"!
Taryn shook her head with a grin and turned around to see the Musician with his bass guitar in
one hand and a bottle of red wine with a purple bow on it in the other hand. He steps up the
stairs and gives her a warm hug.

"Merry Christmas, Taryn," he whispers in her ear.
"Merry Christmas my darling," she replied. Thank you so much for coming."
More and more guests arrive. Taryn goes back inside and closes the big wooden cabin door
behind her. Hangs up her cloak and checks her makeup in a small mirror hanging next to the
door. She turns and smiles at the site of her guests sitting under and around the tree, giggling,
chatting, taking pictures, and shaking gifts and guessing what's inside just like giddy children.
Taryn walks over to the bar and orders a glass of perfectly chilled Moscato. She clinks a fork to it
to get everyone's attention.

"Thank you all for coming to help me celebrate such a wonderful time of year on this cold
blustery night, I love you all so much. Now, just a quick itinerary of the night, First, I'd like to
take a giant selfie of all of us. Jay, did you bring your selfie stick?"
As he is guzzling a glass of champagne, Jay gives a thumb up.

"Great, replies Taryn". Next, we feast in the dining room. Afterwards, we open presents with
wine and assorted drinks of your choice. We may even cut a little rug to some of my favorite
naughty songs. I'll even bust out the bubble machine. Bear, I know how much you love the

bubble machine!"

Everyone laughs and applauses. Bear blushes and waves Taryn away. She continues,
 Umm, and then we'll wind down with opening our stockings. Sounds good to everyone?"
Everyone stands and claps again and whoops and hollers.
"Now, everyone get in tight for this magnificent selfie."
Taryn gathers everyone up in front of the Christmas tree. Jay is trying to fit everyone in,
dictating to squeeze in tighter, and tighter! Taryn poses with one hand on her hip and a glass of
wine in the other.

Jay yells, here we go! Everyone scream Merry Christmas! They all follow his direction and at the
top of their lungs yell, "Merry Christmas!"
Selfie stick replies," CLICK!"
Making her way to another doorway, Taryn states,
 "Alright! Everyone to the dining room! Foods getting cold"! She quickly stops everyone.
"Please find an outlet and charge your phones for the rest of the night. I've hired a
photographer to cover the whole night. So you won't need your phones.......until ......later. She
winks. Let's feast!"

Just light appetizers and desserts span the fourteen person table. Brightly lit red candelabras
decorate the table between each dish. Rumaki, clam dip, assorted cheeses and breads, fruit
kabobs with a cream cheese and yogurt dip, a chocolate fondue garnished with strawberries and
marshmallows, rum cupcakes, and banana cream pie piled high with homemade whipped cream
and sliced bananas.

Small and quiet chit chat, giggles, and flashes from the camera fill the room, as it fills with
warmth, love and heart. After enjoying the essence of the love and seasonal spirit filled room for
a short while, Taryn clinks another champagne glass.
"Now that we have had goodies and treats, everyone full?"
Everyone applauded and rubbed their plump bellies.

Now we commence back to the living room to open presents and enjoy assorted wines and
drinks of your choice. So, I'll see you in a bit," she said with a wink and disappeared behind a
mysterious door.

As the party moved into the living room, they noticed mistletoe had been strung from the
ceiling wall to wall, corner to corner. The photographer was in his glory capturing Taryn's guests
figuring one, it was mistletoe, two; to remind each other they were at a Taryn experience and to
always follow directions, and three; execute.

The Musician sat back in a corner with a gin and tonic at his feet slowly strumming
"This Christmas", a favorite of Taryn's by the brilliant Mr. Donny Hathaway.
The bartender stands on a bar stool, points to the mistletoe and yells,
 "You guys know what to do!!"

The gin and tonic must have gotten through his veins because the Musician stood up, stepped to
the microphone he always traveled with, but before he could open his mouth, there stood at

the top of the staircase, Taryn, in a strapless red dress. She nods her head to continue. She slowly walks down the stairs and The Musician begins

"Hang all the mistletoe I'm going to get to know you better This Christmas"
He sits back and strums his bass instrumentally as Taryn approaches him.
"Such an angelic voice", she compliments.
He nods his head as a thank you.

Taryn orders a glass of Stella Rosa Red Wine and watches everyone open gifts, smooch each other, point at the mistletoe, and watches Bouncer Bear sneak up behind her, wraps one giant arm around her tiny little waist, and kisses her on the cheek. She grabs a hold of his arm and smiles a beautiful smile, and leans back against his enormous body dressed in an ugly sweater, gold chain, and jeans. Photographer captures the whole moment of endearment. Still behind her, he waves a set of keys in front of her face. She grabs them and turns to face him with a look of confusion.

"They are the keys to "The Watering Hole", Merry Christmas baby doll, I'll still run security. I know it's in good hands with you. Make that money, baby."
Welling up with tears, Taryn buried her small body into his huge frame as he wraps one arm around her. The Musician arrives back at the microphone.  Everyone applauses or raises a glass.
"And as we trim the tree, how much fun it's going to be together this Christmas"
Then back to the background strumming instrumentally once again.

Bouncer Bear pulls away and joins Tabitha at the fireplace, camera flashing everywhere. Tabitha suddenly exclaims,
"My turn, my turn!"
Tabitha goes and stands next to her identical looking cousin. All male party guests readjust themselves, gulp mixed drinks, or cover their lap with a present. T&T are a site to see.
"T, from me to you, says Tabitha as she slowly hands Taryn a small purple gift bag. Taryn opens it. She raises the gift high above her head.

"Oh Tabby, replied Taryn in awe. You didn't have to", she gasped.
Abruptly, Jay stands up, obviously drunk,
"Well what the hell is it for us queers up here in the nosebleed section?!?!?"
Both Ken dolls yanked him down without skipping a beat.
"It's a matching diamond choker like Tabby's, exclaimed Taryn. Thank you so much."
"Oh you are so welcome cousin!" Tabby replied with a warm bouncy hug.
"Fireside's blazing bright we're caroling through the night, this Christmas will be a very Special Christmas for me"
"A toast, says Tabitha as she raises her glass. "To my cousin, Taryn", who brings out the very best in all of us, camera flash, everyone raises their glass, including Taryn.
"To Taryn!!!!" the party called out.
Taryn clinks her glass with her cousin. Wiping away tears,
Taryn replies," "More presents!!!"
She grabs assorted size gift bags and gift boxes and hands them out one by one with a pearly white smile.

"Presents and cards are here! My world is filled with joy, cheer and you this Christmas"
New platinum cuff links, white gold chains, white elbow length gloves with a tiara, twin
matching dark blue suede pea coats for next winter, a full expense paid trip to the 2017
Professional Chauffeur's Convention, black leather bound lyric book and brand new matching
gold and black bass guitar, new Timberlands boots, keys to a new Charger, and matching green
baby t-shirts that read "Kiss me and my hot twin sister, I'm Irish".
Many other gifts are given out by Taryn, everyone is getting tipsy and the bartender can hardly
keep up. Taryn quietly slips away and gently presses the power button on the bubble machine
and the play button on her Pandora playlist. She winks at the photographer. He prepares his
lenses just in time to catch Bouncer Bear chase the bubbles. Everyone doubles over in laughs
but race to move out of his way. Photographer is in full swing with his clicks and flashes.
Everyone stands up and begin to groove. Monroe sits quietly and snaps his finger. The Irish
Twins have pulled their hair back into ponytails and pull The Musician between them and begin
to grind against him. Bouncer Bear is spanking Tabitha on her ass as she attempts to twerk. Jay
is drinking straight from a champagne bottle and two stepping as his twin Ken dolls boogie
around him. The Goatee is spinning Taryn around like a ballerina and then grabs her by the waist
and dips her, all to fun music being piped through the surround sound speakers, George Michael
(R.I.P.) tells the party

"Sex, It's natural, It's chemical, It's logical, Habitual, It's Sensual But most of all….. Sex is
something we should do Sex is something for me and you"

Taryn and her party continue to switch dance partners and participate in very provocative dirty
dancing type moves to even nastier songs like to her theme song
"Little Red Corvette" by Prince (R.I.P.),
 "Let's Talk About Sex,"
"Give It to Me Baby" by Rick James (R.I.P.),
 In The Closet, and the ultimate,
"Don't Stop until You Get Enough" by Michael Jackson (R.I.P.)
After the last song, everyone is out of breath but happy and very drunk.
Taryn slowly leads everyone back to the dining room and offered cool towels and bottled water
for a cool down session. But the dining room is noticed to be a little…..different. The long table
is still there. Everyone is instructed to sit where their stocking is.  Then to empty the contents
onto the table (follow the little picture map on the Christmas card so everything is set up
properly which included their cell phones, fully charged. Some guests seem reluctant and
hesitant where others are slapping each other high fives. Another instruction, on a note card,
write down whom at the party they'd like to…..get to know more…..explore. There is neither
shame nor embarrassment. Flip upside down next to the set up in front of you. Next is to roll up
one sleeve if not sleeveless or shirtless already (after that party). Finally to close their eyes,
lights are dimmed and candles lit. Taryn walks into the dining room wearing a deep purple satin
nightgown. Hair is pinned up.

The photographer follows her. She politely stops him and states,
 "The sexiest mindscape is that the privacy and discretion of someone's inner most desires being
shared amongst one another without necessarily capturing it is a turn on naturally."
 She slowly walks to him face to face her breath is steady and soft, his erratic she gently brushes
her hand against the bulge in his jeans. Playing innocent,

"Whoops, I am so sorry. So are you with us? Or can't you part from the camera?"
He leaves the camera in a back room and joins the table.

She slowly blindfolds each guest one after another. She observes the layout of the dining room.
Large body pillows, blankets, and oversized bean bags satisfied. She began,
"Everyone relax, breathe softly and gently, you are safe. There is nothing to be embarrassed or
ashamed of in this room tonight. Tonight I free you. From whatever binds you. "
She kisses everyone on the side of their temple as she reads each card in front of each guest to
herself. She starts with Monroe. She ties a red ribbon around his arm, pokes, pulls back, a red
Christmas, infiltrates, and loosens the ribbon. Once everyone has been set free, she removes the
blindfolds. Taryn stands at the end of the table and quietly says,
"If you see your dream guest. Someone you are so curious about and not ashamed, take that
person to some pillows and blankets anywhere in this room. Share your world, explore
internally and externally, you must hurry. It only lasts 5 minutes. Oh, and take your phones,
these are the moments to capture." Monroe stands and walks in between the Irish Twins opens
both of his arms in offering to escort them. They both giggle and shake their heads yes. Bouncer
Bear turns on the swag and takes Tabitha by the hand, she accepted with wide eyes. He then
throws her over his shoulder as she giggles. Jay of course leads his Ken dolls to a corner.
Everyone is finding a partner and a spot on some pillows. The moaning begins, also begins the
sounds of the panting and kissing echoing against the stone walls.

The Musician and the Thug both stand behind her on opposite sides, one kissing her neck, the
other pulling down the straps to her teddy. The Musician walks in front of her, takes her by the
arm, and kneels before her the Thug follows suit. She realizes what is about to happen. The
moaning is filling the room, louder and louder it gets grunts and moans become almost beastly.
Cufflinks walks up behind Taryn she can feel his large bulge as he bends her head to the side and
kisses it passionately. She closes her eyes suddenly she feels not just two pokes in each arm but
a third in her neck. As the triple bell ringer brings her to her knees, her three suitors lower her to
the dining room table. The Thug enters her first off of memory that she's the tightest with a bell
ringer. The Musician tastes her breasts and all of their fullness. Cufflinks runs his fingers through
her hair and licks her ear lobes then nibbling on them. Bouncer Bear, Monroe, Tabitha, Jay, The
Irish Twins, Ken Dolls, and every other guest all make their way to the dining room table for the
show's finale. Touching themselves or each other, licking fingers, pulling hair, back scratching,
toe curling climaxes and accompanying screams, groans, and panting. All touching Taryn,
caressing all ends of her heavenly body, tasting her juices and smelling her scent.

A very red Christmas.
Merry Christmas from the cabin in the middle of nowhere.

# Extra! Extra! Extra!

*A slew of heartbreak and distress across the city.......*

Detective William Northrup has been hired to follow a Miss Taryn Hart, Case#1695362, with directions to follow and note her every move.

At his desk, Detective Northrup is reading up on Taryn's file. Where she hangs out, who she dines with, even her shopping schedule. His secretary places a fresh cup of coffee on his desk, as something catches her eye, a picture of Taryn having drinks with friends she turns pale and looks like she had just seen a ghost.

"Mr. Northrup, I don't usually comment on any of your cases, but I know this woman." She slowly picks up the picture and quietly studies it.

"Oh?" replies Northrup.

Yes, well, not exactly, replies his secretary, I know of her, I've always heard the rumors about her. They say to lock up your sons and husbands when she comes to town. Because once she's gotten what she wants, she jumps into her black charger and rides out of town, leaving many behind dazed and confused. Detective, you must stop this femme fatale before it's too late."

"Well, I'll do what I can," replied Northrup as he scratches his head.

In all of the years of solving mysteries, he realizes he'd never chased after a femme fatale, did they even exist? Where do you even start? He has the address to her apartment and a camera and decides to park in her apartment complex's parking lot, recline the driver seat back, and wait to see if she arrives or leaves. Not sooner than five minutes, a black Charger came screaming into the parking lot kicking up gravel, and burns rubber into a parking space. Detective Northrup sits up and watches through binoculars. She's wearing simple jeans, white tee shirt, and a black leather jacket. As he looks on, he sees her disappear behind a door that he believes leads to a staircase. He sits up completely and fiddles with his camera. About forty minutes later she exits the apartment building and is heading for her car. Through his lens, he sees she's changed into a black halter top mini cocktail dress and black stiletto heels. He snaps twenty pictures a frame. The chase is on. He mentally notes the make and model of the subject's car, 2015 Dodge Charger, black, license plate MOONCHYLD. To keep up with her he must drive well over 90 mph. She doesn't seem to be phased by the fact that she is speeding way over the speed limit. He passes her cautiously. He sees her in his rearview mirror. He looks down to the passenger seat to grab his camera, only to look up and realize she was gone.

The next day, Northrup rises early with only one thing on his mind, which is capturing this beautiful beast. He starts off by knocking on doors of private homes and businesses flashing a photo of the suspect in question. He was floored by some of the answers and reactions by people once asked about her. He decides to question a few men first and then women on a separate account. He had a hunch he'd be safer with that plan.

"She'll be your dream girl," stated a neighbor working under the hood of his car.

"I just went to go get cigarettes and a Slurpee one night, she almost came out of nowhere in the parking lot. We ended up back at her place, she did things my wife would never do. Trust me," added another neighbor sipping on a can of beer.

"Yeah, but when she's done, she just walks away. She steals your heart then you never see her again," adds the mailman.

"You're never the same again", replied the milkman.

"She leaves you with a void in your heart and in your pants!" added Lionel, the local town drunk. After he finished taking notes, he thanked each man by shaking his hand. Lionel tightened his grip and pulled Detective Northrup in closer and whispered,

"Be careful, she'll get you too, mark my words!"

Northrup is back in his car and thought to himself "lunch was a great idea". It was a lot to take in, parked across the street from the deli shop, Northrup takes a bite of his hot ham and cheese sandwich when low and behold, he sees Taryn coming out of a Starbucks holding a tall green and white cup and heading for her black Charger. She is wearing dark sunglasses, hair in a ponytail, holy jeans, and a purple hoodie. He drops his sandwich and gets his binoculars tangled up with his tie just in time to see she'd made an illegal U-turn. Now she's back on the opposite side of the street passing right by him, her stereo blaring Prince's "Little Red Corvette". He quickly drops the now untangled binoculars, grabs his camera, and snaps as many pictures until she's out of sight.....again!

Frustrated, Northrup decides to interview a few women regarding the ever moving target.

"My husband hasn't been the same since she's been in town!" exclaimed Mrs. Lang, owner of Kut&Kute Beauty Salon.

"Well mine is acting peculiar," started yoga instructor Leah at Blessed Be Yoga and Meditation Center. He just signed up for my yoga class. He claims it's never too late to get in tuned with one's self."  "Wherever she came from, she can turn around and go right on back to wherever it is she came from," replied Rhonda, cashier at the Pic&Save Grocery Store.

If nothing else, many doors were slammed shut in his face by pissed off wives in fuzzy robes, hair curlers, green avocado mud cream masks, and hollering babies on their hips.

 "Umm" Thank you ladies for your time," replied Northrup as he wipes sweat from his brow. Back at his office, the sun has set and the moon is full. Detective Northrup was going over his notes, spotted locations, photos, and not to mention the mixed testimonies of the townsfolk of Blissfield, USA.

"Who are you?" he thought out loud. What's the hype? You have this town flipped upside down, it's like you're a beautiful nightmare."

He unbuttons the first few buttons of his long sleeve shirt and loosens his tie. He suddenly feels warm. He walks to the window, opens it, and inhales the dark and moonlit night. He pulls a handkerchief from his back pant pocket and wipes his face dry. Suddenly his office goes completely dark. Just the moonbeams shine through. He draws his gun and aims at the shadow standing at the doorway. He can hear his heart pounding in his ears. His voice is a little shaky but firm nonetheless.

"Freeze!" Stay right where you are!"

 Suddenly a soft voice cuts through the room.

She giggles and says, "I've been called many things in my time, but never a beautiful nightmare" There's a pause between the two.

 "I like it," she replies as she takes another step.

 Detective Northrup takes another step as well.

 "Dammit I said freeze!" screamed Northrup.

She takes three more steps and presses her cleavage against the drawn firearm. His breath becomes erratic hers stays calm, quiet, and steady.

"What are you going to do, Detective? Shoot me?" she asks.

Northrup can hardly hold his hand steady. He finally lowers his gun he can smell her Obsession perfume. He feels around for the light switch then flips the light on, and turns to see she was

already sitting in the chair opposite of his. She is wearing black stiletto heels, a black pencil shaped skirt with a slit on the left side, and a purple satin button up blouse. Her hair is down with big and wavy curls with a purple clutch purse to match. The white calla lily broach on her blouse matches the barrette pinned in the middle of her hair.

He slowly walks back to his desk but never taking his eyes off of her.

"You're quite the toast of the town, Taryn, is it?" he asks as he lowers to his chair.

"That's my name," she replied in a soft voice.

"I've been looking for you," replied Northrup.

"I know," she answered staring into his eyes.

"And how do you know that?" he asks letting his curiosity get the best of him. She sighs,

"Detective Northrup, would you like to get on with your investigation so we can get on with our lives. I'm a very busy woman."

Filing through his notes and photos he replies,

"I'd say you've been very busy."

He tosses the photos across the desk so she can get a closer look. To humor him she lowers her eyes and glances at the candid shots of herself.

"You've got this whole town flipped upside down, Northrup started as he leans back in his chair. The men have been left dazed and confused they don't know rather to scratch their watch or wind their ass."

She interrupts by slowly saying," But satisfied, I'm sure.

"Then there are the women!" My goodness! It's like ....they love.....to hate you."

"Yes. I get that a lot," she says as she glances out of the window.

Northrup stands from his chair and asks,

"So? What gives? What's the hype of the all mighty sexy siren femme fatale?!?" he asks with exaggerated circus like hand gestures.

Still cool as a cucumber, Taryn replies,

"Detective I am nothing more than a simple female who has the power to seduce anyone at any time, night or day, rain or shine. Is it a crime to bring passion to one's dull and listless life? Every single one of those men was a consenting adult, with their own trials and tribulations, boundaries with the need of a void to be filled. It's human nature, not a crime. As for being pegged a "beautiful nightmare", Detective Northrup," she stands up and saunters over to his side of his desk. She stops and stands behind him then leans over until her lips are millimeters from his ear lobe. The scent of her perfume is captivating; he is frozen in his seat.

I can't help but to take that as a term of endearment." She brings her voice to a breathless whisper,

"A beautiful nightmare". Yes I can accept that. She eases her way to the front of him. She straddles him and wraps her arms around his neck. Looking into his hazel eyes, she says,

"Now that you have your suspect in question, what are you going to do with me, Detective? Tell me."

Detective Northrup squeezes her hips. Taryn tightens her grip around his neck. He tries his hardest not to fall under her spell. But her scent is gripping his sense of smell. He does not want to give into her force. She begins to nibble on his earlobe. She can feel the bulge enhancing in his khakis. Not able to stick to his guns anymore, he stands to his feet lifting her along the way. He props her up onto his desk and slides his hands under her blouse. She throws her head back and melts as his cold and frigid hands warm and adhere to her skin. She pulls him into her. The passion between the two heroes bubbles over into unbuttoning of shirts, lifting of skirts, and dropping of boxer shorts. With one arm, he sweeps across his desk sending files and photos flying into the air. He lays her on her back and lifts one of her knees and enters her full force. Their bodies moved to the rhythm of lovemaking. He kisses her beautiful breasts as she grips the edge of his desk. His movements quicken and his moaning gets louder as he reaches his climax. She meets him at the corner of toe curling and ecstasy with her own body leaving both of them quivering and breathless.

The next morning, Detective William Northrup is finishing up his final statement and conclusion on Case#1695362.

Thursday June 23rd, 2015, 9:15am

<u>Case file# 1695362</u>

After a seven day tailing of a Miss. Taryn Hart, I, Detective William Northrup, Badge #271963, found no physical evidence of heartbreak and or, distress as accused by the townsfolk of Bliss, USA, committed by subject named above as such I conclude, no further investigation is recommended.

**Detective William Northrup**

Detective Northrup tidies up his desk and places case#1695362 in the "case closed" files cabinet. He puts on his hat and trench coat, turns the light off, and closes the door, whistling "Little Red Corvette".

*Finis*

Shanna Bryant was born in Detroit, Michigan and now resides in Greenville, SC. She is the eldest of 6 siblings, 3 brothers and 3 sisters. She is a very proud Aunt to two handsome nephews, and two beautiful nieces. She is very family oriented, with no children of her own; Shanna has a handful of Godchildren and friends who see her as a mother figure.  She has been writing since a very young age. Shanna is a Certified Nurse Assistant, a title she has held in very high regard for over 14 years. Her hobbies include writing, reading, hosting and coordinating theme oriented parties, dancing, bonfires, cooking, working out, collecting Michael Jackson, Prince, and I Love Lucy memorabilia in which she has tattoos of all three celebrities as a true tribute by skin.

She believes she writes the best while under her headphones.

*"I am at my best when surrounded by music"*

*-Shanna Bryant*